UNDERSTANDING GUYS

A Guide for Teenage Girls

MICHAEL GURIAN

Illustrated by Brian Floca

PSS!
PRICE STERN SLOAN

Gurian, Michael.
    Understanding guys: a guide for teenage girls / by Michael Gurian;
    illustrated by Brian Floca.
        p. cm.—(Plugged in)
    Summary: Discusses the emotional, mental, and social differences between males
and females.
    1. Teenage boys—Psychology—Juvenile literature. 2. Teenage girls—
Psychology—Juvenile literature. 3. Interpersonal relations in adolescence—
Juvenile literature. 4. Sex differences (Psychology)—Juvenile literature. [1. Teenage
boys—Psychology. 2. Teenage girls—Psychology. 3. Interpersonal relations. 4. Sex
differences.] I. Floca, Brian, ill. II. Title. III. Series.
HQ797.G87   1998
305.235—dc21   98-41236
                                                                              CIP
                                                                               AC

ISBN 0-8431-7475-7 (pb)   A B C D E F G H I J
ISBN 0-8431-7476-5 (GB) A B C D E F G H I J

For my daughters, Gabrielle and Davita
—M.G.

Acknowledgements
I wish to gratefully acknowledge Jane O'Connor, Emily
Neye, Katrina Weidknecht, the staff of *Price Stern Sloan*,
Susan Schulman, my wife Gail, my children, and all those
young people who have made this book possible.

Contents

INTRODUCTION

Sheri liked athletics, music, some of her classes, and she liked boys. Like practically all her friends, she wondered about guys a lot, what they were thinking, what they were feeling. During her sophomore year Sheri liked a boy named Nathan, but her parents wouldn't let her date yet, so she could only see him in a group of friends.

When she was a junior in high school and she turned sixteen, Sheri was allowed to date. Nathan liked somebody new, but she met another guy whom she really liked, a guy named Jan. He was into sports a little, but even more into music. Sheri could drive now and liked Jan enough to want to see a lot of him and date him seriously.

Sheri had some big decisions now. How much time should she devote to Jan? What should she expect of him? Should she have sex with Jan or not? What should a girl, who is just growing up herself, expect of a guy who is growing up too?

She asked her parents questions, and they helped some, but she wanted to know more. Sheri was a searcher. She wanted to understand things, even the hidden things, that go on between men and women, between teenaged girls and guys.

I met Sheri because I came to speak at her high school. After the class discussion, I started talking with Sheri and the other young women. Sheri asked me very specific questions about what goes on in a boy's head and in his heart.

"What are boys thinking and feeling?" she asked. "What do they want?"

"Why do they go so blank?" another girl asked.

"Why do they talk on and on about worthless things?" someone else asked.

"Are they really different from us? Or is it just how they were raised?"

"What do they want?"

The questions were wonderful. So was the discussion we had, even though I didn't have all the answers. It was after that day I decided to write this book on what I *do* know about guys. I decided to write a book for girls and young women like Sheri searching for answers to important questions about adolescent boys.

Let me tell you about myself. I am the father of two daughters who are still young yet—six and nine. I am also a therapist and have spent a large part of my professional life studying boys—why they behave the way they do, how they become men, and what it means to be masculine. I've lived in a number of different places—Israel, Turkey, Germany, India—and watched how other cultures bring up their teen girls and boys. I've written a lot of books for adults on how kids develop and how love works between men and women.

From my experience, I have come to view attraction between adolescents as important in the lives of the two young people involved, and also as important in the life of the whole community. The kinds of relationships you are in now, or soon will be in, are like lifeblood both to you and to your community. The love you experience for a boy is like breathing. That is how important it is, in my opinion. If you can really understand someone else's mind and heart, especially when that mind and heart are quite different from yours, you can communicate much better and love someone more completely.

Sometimes high-school students will say, "Wait a minute. There's no difference between girls and guys, or if there is, it's because society tries to make us different." Although in many ways that's true, once we scratch the surface, there are immense differences, differences that show up both in fun and painful ways. And lots of these differences show up in girls and guys no matter the culture or society they live in.

I've written this book because I believe that Sheri and millions of other girls can have better relationships with boys, if they understand what's happening inside boys. God knows, a boy often won't tell a girl, will he! But it doesn't have to remain a complete mystery. This book is about the inner life of a boy, what he's thinking and feeling.

Let me say that sometimes I'll refer to you as a girl and other times as a woman or young woman. Sometimes I'll refer to guys as boys and other times as young men or men. Since this book is written for adolescents between fourteen and eighteen, some of you are still girls and some of you have become women already. Some of the guys you know are still boys and some truly are men now. As you're reading, fill in the word that best fits yourself or the guys you know.

I'm going to talk a lot about hormones and the brain as well as conditioning or socialization (the ways society tells us to act). I will generalize about "girls" and "boys" or "men" and "women." Not for a minute do I mean that all girls or all boys, all men or all women are a certain way. I only mean that there are very strong tendencies among the majority of either sex to think and feel in certain ways.

Learning about these tendencies is often, for many teens, like finding out the secret language of love and friendship. If you don't learn the secret language, love and friendship with the other sex can be so much more difficult. But if you do, you'll be much better able to love and be loved by someone.

In these pages, I will only discuss emotional, mental, and social differences between males and females that I have seen to exist in our culture and in cultures all over the world. If it's in this book, you can trust I have seen it over and over again in people and in studies from all over the world.

Watch out how you use this stuff. Once you learn about these differences, don't use what you know to cut someone down, or to humiliate another person. A girl might say, "Yeah, see, that's just how the male brain is. . ." and add some insult. Or a guy might say, "Yeah, see, I always knew girls were. . ." and get in some dig. Maybe I'm crazy, but I think the secrets inside each of us are so important that we need to treat them with deep respect.

I remember Sheri and her friends and the other girls at that school as searchers after the hidden truths inside all of us. I hope this book explains some of those truths to you.

CHAPTER 1

Why Boys
Are the Way They Are

$\mathcal{D}$oes this conversation sound familiar?

She: Why did you get a tattoo? You and your friends just have to prove something all the time.

He: What are you talking about? We're just being guys. It looks cool.

She: You're nuts.

How about this one?

He: Okay, I see I should have called to say I'd be

late, but is it so important that you have to keep talking about it?

She: I'm just trying to get you to understand, to get you to hear me.

He: I hear you. I hear you. Let's just drop it.

Or this one?

She: What's so important about that car? You treat it better than you treat me.

He: It's a '66 Chevy with a dual cam engine. You wouldn't understand.

She: It's just a car!

This one?

He: Are you coming to the game tonight?

She: We were going to my cousins' party, remember?

He: Oh yeah. Forgot. Sorry. But I can't miss the game.

If you don't already have a boyfriend, pretty soon you will become involved in a close relationship with a teenaged guy who will, after the first few weeks of romantic infatuation are over, drive you nuts sometimes. He'll drive you nuts for reasons that this book can't cover. He'll also drive you nuts for some reasons this book *can* cover: If you learn how to deal with differences between you, your relationship doesn't become just a power struggle between a boy and a girl in their middle teens.

As a man who was once a teenaged boy, I know this from experience: Many problems in romances grow out of the fact that boys are so different from girls.

 In this chapter, I want to give you X-ray vision into the inner workings of teen boys so you can see the ways in which boys are different. Your bodies are different, sure, but there's a lot more that's different: Your hormones are different and your brain structures are different. Hormones and brain structures determine a lot of human behavior, so naturally you and the boys you know are different sorts of people.

TESTOSTERONE: THE DRIVING FORCE IN EVERY GUY

There is a powerful hormone in a boy's body called testosterone. Testosterone is the male hormone that a boy's brain signals his testicles to create and flood into his bloodstream. It controls a lot of what makes him a man. We'll talk a lot about it throughout this book because it affects how his body changes, how he feels about sex, what some of his moods and emotions are like, as well as the way he behaves toward you and others in his life.

Not only does testosterone make a boy grow taller and fill out his muscles, but testosterone is a sex and aggression hormone. In other words, it exists in great part to make the body of the boy want to be aggressive and want to have sex.

Until puberty, it is as if a boy's body has been through a long winter. Snow has been falling in the mountains for ten years or more. A lot of snow has accumulated up there. When puberty starts, the snow starts to melt and floods into all the streams and rivers in his body. The flooding remains really heavy for the two to four years of puberty, and it keeps flowing pretty strongly until the boy is a man in his late forties or fifties—your dad's age or older. At this time, the flow of testosterone has lessened, and by the time he is in his seventies or eighties—your grandfather's age—the amount of testosterone will be a much smaller stream.

Adolescence is the time of the strongest flood, and it creates great imbalances: His body is flooding with testosterone but his mind isn't yet clear on how to manage it.

A teenaged boy gets between five and seven surges or "peaks" of testosterone flow through his body every day. What's the effect of all this? He'll probably bump into things and seem clumsy at times. He most likely feels like masturbating a lot because testosterone creates a great deal of tension inside his body, especially sexual tension, and masturbation releases it. He'll start fantasizing sexually about girls and thinking about how to get sex. He may get into more fights (or at least act more aggressive, maybe in sports). Even a boy who isn't a jock or quick to get in fights may find himself liking more aggressive video games and movies. He may want to take you to Arnold Schwarzenegger movies when you might have absolutely zero interest.

He may egg on friends to do things that are risky—dangerous things, like driving a car too fast, or immoral things, like stealing.

All these things can have a lot to do with the testosterone surges in his body. By the time he is sixteen or so, his testosterone level will be twenty times greater than the level of testosterone in the body of a sixteen-year-old young woman.

All the behavior described above can apply to girls too—plenty of girls are aggressive, play sports, like to masturbate, want sex, enjoy violent movies, do immoral things. However, all over the world, adolescent boys tend to behave in these ways more often than adolescent girls. And testosterone is a big reason why.

Some boys have extra-high levels of testosterone. You can generally tell high-testosterone boys by these clues:

- they are very into aggressive sports, like football
- they are very focused on getting sex as much as possible
- they are very ambitious—for example, wanting to start their own software company at age seventeen.

Other boys have lower testosterone levels than the average male. These boys tend to be a little more contemplative, not as active, not as hard-driven. They tend to avoid highly aggressive activities. They may have slightly lower sex drives.

A boy's testosterone level is not the measure of manliness. High-testosterone boys are no more "manly" than low-testosterone boys. Often high-testosterone boys pretend they're more "a man" than low-testosterone boys, but it's not true. They're just showing off. We're just getting fooled if we think the amount of testosterone flowing through a guy's body is a measure of his manhood.

FEMALE HORMONES

If you react differently from the boys you know, hormones are one of the reasons. Female hormones—estrogen and progesterone—make a young girl's body develop into a woman's body able to become pregnant and give birth.

Female hormones also cause women to bond with their newborn baby. If you get pregnant some day, the level of progesterone in your body can increase to one hundred times its normal level. Progesterone is called "the bonding hormone." A helpless newborn needs lots of love and care, so nature is very smart to make a female hormone that causes women to feel such intense love for their babies.

Males don't have much of this hormone, just as girls don't have nearly as much testosterone. The male's lack of progesterone further complicates the problem of teen pregnancy in our culture. Teenaged guys don't have a hormonal bond with their newborn baby. Teenaged girls do, and so they end up taking care of the child. In over ninety percent of cases of teen pregnancy, the mother is abandoned by her boyfriend. For males to bond with a child, they have to form a long-term emotional bond with the mother and child. Most teen males are not capable of doing this the way teen girls are.

A BRIEF HISTORY OF HUMAN DEVELOPMENT

How did things get set up this way? Once I was talking to a group of girls and one of them—a tall, very athletic seventeen-year-old—said, "It's not fair! The guy gets to wander around doing what he pleases, and we get stuck with the responsibilities."

If you've felt this, you're not alone, though when you look at male/female makeup objectively, you'll find advantages to being female, too. More on this later.

As far as basic biological identity, things got set up the way they are for boys and girls because of millions of years of human development. Our prehistoric ancestors lived in communities where the goal was survival. The world was a very scary place, filled with predatory animals and natural disasters. The human race needed to protect itself by staying physically strong. Women were built especially to bear children and so developed more fat than muscle mass. Often they had to have ten kids for just a couple to survive into adulthood. Men were built to hunt and so developed larger muscle mass.

Women didn't need to develop a very high sex drive, because once they became pregnant, there was no need for them to have sex for another nine months. Mother Nature gave males a higher sex drive so they could get lots of women pregnant; there would be lots of children; and the species would survive.

Until around thirty thousand years ago, men and women had sex without being in a family unit. The woman ovulated; the males competed among each other (often fighting) in order to have sex with the fertile woman. She might have sex with many males during her fertile time. Once she got pregnant and gave birth, the whole community helped care for the child because no one really knew exactly which man had fathered it.

Over the few million years humans have been a species, women needed more and more estrogen and progesterone while men needed more testosterone, so the levels of these hormones have increased in us. Once a young woman said to me, "Why do girls still need so many female hormones now? Life is not such a fight to survive, and we know who our kids' fathers are." Her point was, Look, nobody's fighting woolly mammoths anymore. And kids are raised in families with moms, dads, grandparents, and close friends. Women don't need to have as many kids as they used to because modern medicine is helping all human beings live longer.

Well, she was right about all this. However, one of the strongest forces controlling sex hormones in our bodies is competition that results from today's high population growth. The more people there are on the planet competing for food, clothing, shelter, medicine, money, and everything else, the more our bodies create hormones that help us compete. Males get more testosterone so they can compete better in society. Females get more progesterone so they can bond even more strongly with their own offspring.

And the increases in hormones cross over between the sexes too. For instance, girls today have more testosterone than females did thirty thousand years ago. The result is they are somewhat more aggressive than their female ancestors. We may well discover soon that males today are getting a little more progesterone in their systems than they used to. The hormonal systems in us as a species are always making slight adjustments.

When you watch your own body, you're witnessing millions of years of history. When you watch boys acting the way they act, you're watching millions of years of development. It's like a mirror reflecting our very beginnings.

And of course, hormones don't account for all the differences between guys and girls. Society does play a big part. Societies see that, by nature, boys tend toward more physical aggression and competition and so societies teach them to be more aggressive. Often, boys are not taught when it's inappropriate to be aggressive, and so they can overwhelm other people. If you've been in a classroom, trying to get the teacher to notice you, but the boys are shouting out, raising their hands all the time, you've noticed how this can work. You, as a girl, can feel lost in the background.

Society sees that girls tend to be less physically aggressive, and so girls are not taught things like self-defense, or competitiveness in sports, or ambition in the workplace, and girls' self-esteem suffers. Our society is just learning about what's actually going on inside boys and girls, how to understand what's going on without stereotyping boys and girls, and how to make sure that, as much as possible, all children have equal opportunities to succeed in whatever way they need to.

YOUR AVERAGE MALE BRAIN

If testosterone is the hidden energy source of teen boys, the way the male brain is formed determines how a boy organizes that energy. Testosterone plus a male brain explains, in large part, what makes boys the way they are. I see adolescent boys as part warrior and part artist. The warrior part of the boy comes from his testosterone. The artist part comes from his brain. You'll see what I mean.

The male brain has been developing for a few million years, just as the female brain has been developing in its way. There are a lot of similarities between these two brains, but also differences.

If you're surprised by the terms "the male brain" and "the female brain," you're not alone. Many people don't realize that a teen boy's brain and a teen girl's brain are somewhat different. Many people don't want to accept it. They prefer to say, "Any differences between boys and girls arise from society, which teaches these differences. We're really alike."

This is not true. Just as the structure of your body is different from the structure of a boy's body, so is the structure of your brain. Right now, some researchers who study the brain have found seven structural differences between the male and female brain. These differences are apparent in adolescence and have a lot to do with how you relate to boys and they to you.

Having said all this, it is important to remember that there isn't just one "male brain" and one "female brain." There is much variety among male brains and female brains. There are many ways that you as a girl can be very "male" and boys you know can be very "female." The human brain is an amazing organism that adapts very well from generation to generation. At the same time, the male brain and the female brain do have certain tendencies—different tendencies—you ought to know about.

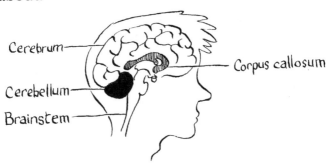

CROSS-SECTION of THE BRAIN

If we put on our X-ray glasses and could look into a boy's head and a girl's head, what are some differences we would see in their brains?

We would notice that the boy's brain is, on

average, about ten percent larger than the girl's brain. This doesn't make it better or worse, just different.

We would notice that within the smaller female brain is a larger corpus callosum than in the larger boy's brain. The corpus callosum is the bundle of nerves that connects the brain's right and left hemispheres.

We would notice that the female brain produces more serotonin than the male brain does. Serotonin is kind of like a chemical in the brain; it inhibits aggressive behavior. On average, boys have less serotonin in their brains. This helps explain why they can be loud, obnoxious, drive faster, take more physical risks, act so competitively, etc.

We would also notice differences in the way girls and boys use the right and left hemispheres of the brain. At a number of universities, brain-scan equipment is being used to reflect what parts of the brain males and females use for the same task. Color computer images show results.

When a teen boy and teen girl are asked to work "spatially"—like putting together blocks or some other kind of task involving use of physical space—the right hemisphere of the male brain lights up very dramatically. In a female brain, both hemispheres light up equally, but less colorfully.

Spatial tasks—like working with blocks, fixing a car, or building a house—are processed mainly in the right hemisphere of the human brain. So a brain that produces more right hemisphere activity—and that's a male brain—will on average do better at a lot of those kinds of tasks.

On the other hand, when verbal skills are tested, the computer images from brain scans show the female brain to be, on average, more active. Girls, on average, use more words than boys, and they use more variety in their language. Girls, on average, can say what they are feeling more quickly than boys. Their friendships usually include more words, more conversation.

So, where boys tend to direct themselves more toward physical space (and virtual space, in computers), girls tend to direct themselves more toward "relationship space," or "verbal space," where they can talk things out.

There are always exceptions to this. Some girls are brilliant engineers (a typical spatial activity), or computer geeks, and don't care much for relationships. Some boys are great at talking about feelings and couldn't care less about looking under the hood of a car or doing any

physical sports. And there are mixes of all kinds—guys as well as girls who like spatial and verbal activities equally.

Still, often you'll find that the guy you are making friends with will not be as good as you are at talking about his feelings. If you consider him defective because of this disadvantage, your relationship may not go very far.

At the same time, guys may get overwhelmed by how much talk and other kinds of contact girls need. Just because his brain and his testosterone make him kind of standoffish and independent, he shouldn't consider you weird because of the way your brain works.

In talking about boys and girls, it's important that we always remember that so many differences are in the brain. They aren't differences that are going to go away because we want them to. It's up to you to learn what they are and, hopefully, get guys to learn about them too. That way, relationships can allow both girls and guys to be who they are and meet somewhere in the middle as romantic friends.

YOUR BRAIN AND HIS BRAIN: HOW ARE THEY DIFFERENT?

Just why does the male brain make it harder for boys to talk about feelings and the female brain make it harder for girls to do spatial tasks? The answer, again, goes back to the human development we talked about earlier.

For millions of years, males had to hunt and females had to raise children. Hunting is a spatial activity. An object is moving through space— a deer, a mammoth, a bear. The male must track its movements through space, then zero in for the kill, in order to bring food back to the community. That's how the male brain spent ninety-nine percent of our human history.

In order to be best suited for the survival task of hunting, males developed more muscle mass and less body fat, developed more aggressive, competitive instincts, *and* an ability to calculate direction speed and the distance between objects—all the skills needed to hurl an arrow or spear through space to kill prey. Males did not need to develop a lot of word skills while hunting—talk would make noise and alert the prey. Nor did males need to know a lot about processing complex feelings (there's isn't a great need to relate to others in an emotionally complex way while hunting in the wilderness).

Females, on the other hand, needed to process a lot of feelings in order to care for and love their children and take part in the busy village community life. Instead of aggression and competition, they needed more relationship and conversation—more verbal skills, less spatial ability.

Jumping ahead, say, two million years to your world today, you'll see all this operating right in your own school. Think of the phrase "objects moving through space" and apply it to a lot of what teen (and adult) males spend their lives doing—playing basketball and watching basketball, playing football and watching football, racquetball, tennis, soccer. . . on and on the list goes. Instead of hunting deer, males now hunt balls. They develop communities and teams among themselves to hunt these balls, these objects moving through space.

The same parallel applies to girls today. Look around the school cafeteria. Girls tend more toward long, involved conversations with each other. They tend to enjoy picking up on hidden cues and arguing about hidden agendas among kids. Certainly many boys may listen in and also like to talk and know what's going on with everybody. And certainly many girls play sports as well or better than lots of boys. (Verbal and spatial skills are developed in both male and female brains.) But on average, you'll notice differences in how girls and boys like to spend their time.

Another good example—notice who does what with the remote control of the television. So often, a guy you know will go surfing quickly, switching from object to object, channel to channel, looking for action between objects—fights, car chases—not for a long emotional dialogue between people. More often, a girl will want to find something that has some emotional content, some relationship "stuff." Again, this difference is hard-wired into male/female brains and then, of course, socialized, as males are still encouraged to go for more "action" in life and females for more "relationship."

In a sense, that remote control points up a lot of the difficulties in adolescent boy-girl love. He's going for action, you're going for relationship. There will be exceptions to this—times when he wants to talk and you want to go do something—but more often than not, boys and girls, men and women, lean toward what their brains are wired to do.

So now you understand that testosterone and a different kind of brain system account for much of why boys are the way they are. You see that *males and females often have different abilities as far as dealing with their feelings.* But where does that leave you as far as figuring out how to get along with some guy you like?　Well, understanding boys' emotions helps a lot—and that is the focus of the next chapter.

CHAPTER 2

Guys and Their Emotions: What Are They Really Feeling?

$\mathbb{T}$he scene was a roundtable discussion in a junior year social studies class. There were about twenty-five students, pretty much evenly divided between girls and boys. The topic was gender roles and sex roles. The teacher and I asked the boys to all sit on one side of the room and the girls on the other. Once everyone had moved, we asked how it felt to just be with one's own sex.

First, the answer was "no big deal." But then some of the students began to open up.

"Safer," a girl said. "I feel safer with just the girls."

"Lonely," another girl said. "I feel lonely without my boyfriend sitting next to me."

"Like I can say more and think more freely," another girl said, "because I'll be heard."

"Sad," one girl said. We asked her what she meant. "Sad because I don't want to feel good like this, being just with the girls, but I do feel good."

"Why should it make you sad to enjoy being in the company of the girls?" the teacher asked.

"I guess because I want everything to be the same whether I'm a girl or a boy, but it's not."

Her comment was very interesting, and also interesting was that none of the boys volunteered to answer the question, "How does it feel to just be with one's own sex?" We had to ask the boys to become involved, and we had to talk a lot of the boys into saying anything.

I've done this exercise with students all over the world and generally what happens is the same. The girls are freer, more verbal, and more open about the emotional understanding of their experiences.

When I pointed this out to these students, one of the boys said: "I don't mind raising my hand or talking in class when I have something to say, but about this stuff, what's there to say?" Hidden in his comment is something very telling. In other circumstances, for instance, during a discussion about a point in a history book that interests him, he can be as verbal as any girl—in fact, some of the girls probably complain that he may be a little too verbal, and can overwhelm the class. But when it comes to an on-the-spot emotional response to a subtle situation, he feels out of his element.

That hour in the social studies classroom showed just the tip of the iceberg as far as revealing the different emotional makeup of teen boys and teen girls (as well as men and women). Some of the difference is socialized, but a lot of it is in the brain and in the hormones.

TESTOSTERONE AT WORK

The hormone testosterone has a profound effect on the way guys process their feelings. Here are some things you need to know before you can have a satisfying emotional life with a young man. (And, once again, remember the young man you know may act differently from what I describe, because the human body, endocrine system, and brain are far more complex than a few pages here can summarize—but his behavior will fall into some of these categories.)

In lots of situations, you'll notice that the boy you are getting to know has a profound emotional disadvantage compared to you or a lot of girls you know. His body is just not set up as well as yours to handle as wide a range of emotions. Let's look at some ways this happens.

Quick Tension Release. A girl and a boy fail the English midterm. The girl is more likely to get a little teary and seek comfort from friends. The boy is more likely to slap the test down on his desk, hit his fists together, curse, and otherwise deal with the stress in his body quickly. He's less likely to cry and look for emotional contact. The girl is more likely to turn the stress of failure into a way of creating emotional closeness.

Testosterone, the aggression hormone, is part of the reason for the different way a boy might react emotionally to the failed test. Testosterone wires the male to react to the pain and anxiety with an aggressive response, a curse or slap of his fist, that helps him release tension quickly and aggressively. Estrogen and progesterone, the hormones that drive you, as a girl, are not aggression hormones. Your hormones make you tend to want *more* emotional contact rather than less. While you are as capable as any guy of being aggressive—of cursing or punching something—you will not tend to respond in this way as much.

So, partly because of their hormones, boys are less likely to use disappointment, sadness, or pain as ways of becoming close to someone else, including you. You've probably noticed that often when boys are suffering emotionally about something going on in their family, they just won't get any help. They won't reach out, they'll remain stoic, they'll pretend everything's fine.

Crying. Think about adolescent males and crying. Teen guys do a lot less crying than they did before puberty. Although acculturation—that's stuff like society saying, "Real men don't cry, so you shouldn't either, son!"—accounts for some of this change, biology is also a very large factor.

There is a hormone in us called prolactin, which is largely responsible for making sure our tear glands grow. Females have more of this hormone than males; girls' tear glands tend to be bigger than boys' after puberty, so their tears flow more freely.

Also, testosterone directs the boy's body to release tension quickly rather than engage in an activity like crying, which prolongs the time spent dealing with the painful situation. If I start to cry, people come around to talk and help and the emotional moment goes on longer than if I just bite my lip and don't cry.

Why does testosterone make a guy behave like this?

Again, think back to what the male was doing for millions of years—hunting and making war. A male couldn't survive if he developed an internal system that made him want to cry a lot. If his buddy next to him died from a lion attack or from an enemy's spear and he started crying, he'd lose his focus and be killed too.

Repression of Feelings. In highly dangerous situations, males learned that a better way to survive was to repress feelings. So, often, a man will tend to release a little of the tension at the moment, but repress more of it and store it up for use later. For instance, the male represses the painful emotions of seeing a friend killed and turns them into anger which he uses to fight back at the enemy even more intensely.

This still happens today, even though guys are not fighting a lion or dealing with an enemy attack on the village. Now if a boy gets hurt—let's say he gets into a fight with his best friend—he may respond by covering up the pain, then two hours later playing a hell of a game of basketball because he's got that stored (repressed) emotional energy to use now.

While everybody—girls and boys—represses feelings sometimes, adolescent boys do it a great deal. When you see a boy you care about who is trying his hardest to avoid crying, it can help to encourage him to cry or talk. But also be aware that he probably will never cry as much now as he did before he hit puberty, and he will probably repress far more feelings than you do. This can be very frustrating for relationships. As you get to know him, you may notice that waiting a few hours, or even a few days, to talk to him about something very emotional can sometimes work.

Dominating Others. Have you noticed how much some adolescent boys try to dominate each other? Have you noticed some of them try to dominate discussions in class? Have you noticed how they try to dominate their girlfriends?

Testosterone is part of the reason some guys act like this. The behavior comes partly from an inborn "territorial" instinct. "This is my territory and don't you forget it." Spitting, a very male behavior, is a kind of territorial behavior, like urinating on a spot was a way of claiming territory in prehistoric times. When you watch a group of guys talking to each other, just fooling around together, you'll notice lots of dominance behavior—"You're full of it," "No way, you don't know anything."

People used to think that guys who tried to dominate were just insecure or immature. While that can be very true, it is also true that the strong flow of testosterone through an adolescent boy's body causes this need for dominance.

Dominance behavior can scare off people who aren't used to it, rather than bringing these people closer together. That is an emotional problem for dominating boys. It puts them in something of an emotional disadvantage. Who wants to be emotionally close to a boy who is trying to dominate others? And while the boy may get others to give in to him or pretend they're giving in, what he's not doing is opening up emotionally. It's harder for him than for the average girl to build a relationship based on mutual trust.

Adolescent girls can get dominating in this way too, but generally it's still more of a "guy" thing.

How should a girl respond to this kind of behavior? There is no easy answer. It takes a long, long time for a lot of guys to learn emotional skills that let them overcome their need to dominate. If you get to know the guy's family and notice that either his mom or dad is very dominating, then he might have an even harder time learning the emotional skills we're talking about. It's good to remember that most high-testosterone adolescent males don't learn how to act differently until they are adults and moving into middle age.

If you are in a relationship with a boy who doesn't try to dominate, you are probably in a relationship with a boy who is not a "high-testosterone male," and/or a boy who has learned from his family and community how to put dominance patterns aside so that he can relate with more emotional depth.

Delayed Reactions. Boys can take a long time to process or sort out their feelings. Studies have been done which compared how long it takes a young man to process emotional reactions to a situation and how long it takes a young woman. One such study showed that young women processed their feelings seven hours earlier than young men.

My grandmother had a funny thing to say to me about this regarding my grandfather. After reading one of my books, she said, "You actually get people to buy your books? You're just saying what we've always known! Look, if I wanted your grandfather to think about something important, I brought it up to him before he went to work and let him think about it, then we talked at supper. I always knew men took longer to think about how they felt!"

What my grandmother did was a smart thing to do. This might work for you too, especially with a boyfriend you've already noticed needs time to "digest" his emotions. Sometimes you have to wait a day or a few days to bring the heavy topic up again and get a clear, useful, loving response.

This makes it difficult, often, for guys and girls to relate. Girls have often processed the emotional content of a situation—an argument, a movie, something that happens among your friends—long before the guy has. You, as a girl, may want to get into talking about it right away. Your boyfriend may not be able to.

Problem Solving. Have you noticed that many boys you know want to put an end to emotionally charged situations as soon as possible? If you're sad, your boyfriend may want to fix what's bothering you, problem-solve it ASAP. Where you may want to keep on being emotional about something, he may not be able to stay there with you, and what he may do, instead, is get angry or pull away.

In the male hormones and brain system, there

is a big push to process emotion "efficiently." To him this often means not getting too caught up in feeling a lot of stuff. It means finishing the problem quickly. Very often, for the male, feeling and expressing a lot of emotion seems dangerous. If someone's "feeling bad," the male drive to "fix it right away" kicks in. This is especially true of guys who've gone through their boyhoods without being taught any other way.

Let's remember that for millions of years it didn't matter much if males didn't "feel" as much as females or "talk about feelings" as much as females. In primitive society, females didn't need males, as a group, to be as emotionally complex as females. Females did most of their emotional processing with other females, not males. Even not so long ago, marriages were arranged; young people did what they were told, married whom they were told to marry, didn't try to "communicate" as much and "be best friends" with their spouses. They didn't worry as much about whether they were in love. The males spent most of their time away from the females, in the company of men—situations that didn't require as much emotional complexity.

A big change has occurred in modern culture but our hormones and brain have remained pretty much the same. The basic hormonal structure of adolescent boys and girls hasn't changed much, but love, romance, intimate marriage matter a lot now; and these sorts of relationships have gone very much in the direction of what fits hormones like progesterone (a bonding hormone) better than what fits testosterone (an aggression hormone). So males now live in a world where the effects of testosterone often work against having the kind of long-term, intimate, emotional relationships that adolescent females' bodies and hormones as well as modern culture often see as ideal.

Think of it this way: Even just a few hundred years ago, society was still arranged so males would protect and provide for females and children, and in return the females and children would give males greater social status. Every family accepted the man's emotional disadvantages in the home, but saw his social advantages in the culture. Adolescent males and females were raised accordingly. This arrangement worked well for millions of years—the standard of success being that the human species survived.

But our culture, (I'm talking about the last one hundred years) has been experimenting with changing this arrangement. Our wealthy culture has gone far beyond just taking care of survival needs. We have the freedom to experiment with new ways of caring for each other and for our human community. You, as young people, are generally being brought up to live in a world where both women and men can be equally independent, and where perhaps the old "gender deal" isn't needed anymore.

Our culture is committed to this idea, but

often that doesn't help us in our intimate relationships too much. In those relationships we find that without compromise, without accepting gender differences, and without some version of a "gender deal," love and intimacy just don't last.

We are, after all, still very much like human beings were hundreds of thousands of years ago. As lovers, a man and a woman are often very different: One is driven to release tension quickly, not cry as much, not process feelings as quickly, become somewhat irritable when too much time is spent on "every little feeling"— and he is often acculturated to see this style of relating as superior; the other is driven to delve deeper into feelings, want more times of one-on-one emotional closeness, and become dissatisfied when her boyfriend won't explore intricate emotions with her.

What compromises are you willing to make in order to love a young man and be loved by him? Before you answer, let's look at some other areas of profound difference between you and a guy you might like. Your boyfriend will probably not fit all of these traits, but he'll fit some.

DIFFERENT BRAINS, DIFFERENT STYLES

Often, guys use one part of their brain for something girls might use three parts of the brain for. Sometimes brain researchers illustrate this by saying that the guy's brain is like a building with separate rooms for separate functions; the female brain is more like a body of water—it spreads out in many places.

For instance, a boy who is busy at a computer may not hear what you are saying because he's using one part of the brain, the seeing part, not the hearing part. Unless you talk loudly, his "hearing part" won't get stimulated and you'll think you're being ignored. A girl is more able to use different parts of her brain at once, so she can "switch gears" between the computer and a conversation more easily. She also tends to get less angry or frustrated when she's concentrating on one task and is interrupted by someone wanting her to focus on something completely different.

It's one of the reasons adolescent girls and women on average score higher on communication and social skills tests than males do, and higher on emotional recognition tests. Their brains are better suited to cross back and forth between the kinds of processing that lots of emotional contact requires.

Because of their brains, females often tend to take in more subtle details of what's going on around them, and remember more of what happened to them; they even test out better than the average male on intuition. Females often end up being better judges of character than males. "He's bad," you might say about a guy in school. "You should avoid him." Your boyfriend doesn't listen, but your intuition turns out to be right.

Sometimes girls can think they are more insecure about relationships than boys are because they talk more about relationships; but, in fact, boys come at relationships with somewhat less developed skills. Their silence may appear as strength, but those guys are usually immensely insecure too.

Words. Every week, you, as an adolescent girl, use on average between three and five times the number of words that an adolescent boy does. From early on and all the way through life, females on average have superior verbal skills, especially about emotional content.

If you're reading this and thinking, "What? I know lots of guys who talk *way* more than I do," you're right. Lots of guys use lots of words. But watch conversations and notice something: To a great extent, they talk mainly about thinking and doing. Listen even more closely and you'll notice that when they talk on and on, it is mainly about projects or goals where they are challenged to show they can do it correctly. For instance, you might ask a boy about his friendship with somebody and hear mainly about what he did with that guy.

When it comes to conversations about *feelings*, adolescent males on average don't use as many words, don't have as much to say. As one sixteen-year-old girl, sitting beside her boyfriend, said at a Healthy Youth conference, "Getting him to talk about how he feels is like taking a kid to the dentist." Some guys are great at using words to speak of feelings—some guys can say, "I was feeling very sad and hurt and vulnerable" and then really get into why, and how. But on average guys just won't talk as much as girls and won't talk as much about some of the very things girls really want to talk about.

The Five Senses. So, we've talked about how you and other girls seem to hear better than a lot of guys. If you watch closely, you may notice that girls tend to smell things with more subtlety, taste with more intensity. You may also notice that girls like to hug and touch each other more. "I've led  camps for girls and camps for boys," one teacher told me. "In the girls' camps, it's like one long sleepover, with girls doing their friends' hair, and so on. In the boys' camps, there's much less touch, and when there is touching, it's quick slaps and things like that."

Maybe you've assumed that these differences in behavior come from boys being told touching each other is bad and girls being told it is good. To some extent, that's so. But also, some of the differences come from hardwiring in the brain. The female brain is wired, generally, to take in more sensory data: More sights, sounds, smells, tastes, and touch. One reason is the female hormone estrogen. It promotes more activity in a lot of the brain cells that are involved in sense perception. You may have experienced this yourself—when, during your menstrual cycle, your estrogen is heightened, your senses may feel *very* alive.

Testosterone and the male brain system tend to focus the guy on specific tasks rather than general sensory experience. In other words, a guy concentrating on working at his computer will pick up on the sounds involved in that task, but may not hear background noise, including whatever you're saying to him.

Often the guy you think is not listening is, in fact, just not hearing. Often the guy who seem uninterested in cuddling or holding hands does not have the highly developed tactile sense you do.

Once a teen girl told me about talking to her boyfriend's mother. She and the mom were saying how her boyfriend wasn't much of a hugger. The mom said, "When he was a kid, he loved to hug me. Then he started growing up and didn't want to anymore. It wasn't cool to hug, I guess." Some of why he stopped hugging was definitely socialization—what he thought was acceptable or cool as a teen. In our culture males are taught not to show much physical affection. But also, once puberty hits, with its surges of testosterone, boys often tend to cut back on the hugging. This doesn't mean you shouldn't hug your boyfriend or encourage him to hug you back. It just means you need to be understanding when he doesn't seem to want the same kind of close contact you do.

This is one of the great frustrations of adolescent relationships. So often, the girl wants more hugging, more soft touching, more flowers to smell, more sweet words than the boy wants or is able to give.

We've gone inside our bodies and our heads and searched for some of the secrets as to why boys and girls are the way they are. Now the question is, how should we deal with these differences? The next chapter is about practical strategies for relating to boys and young men.

CHAPTER 3

Relationships:
Meeting in the Middle

I was teaching boy/girl differences at a boys' school once. This boys' school had a sister school, and so the audience was coed. When I had finished talking about the "flexible," "expansive" female brain and the "task-oriented," "focused" male brain, a young woman, who was a senior at the girls' school, raised her hand.

"You know," she said, "I hate to say it, but doesn't it seem like girls just have better brains than the guys!"

This brought a lot of laughter and also led to

a serious discussion. Some of the boys and young men talked about how they really resented the way I was portraying the male and female brain. Like some of the girls, they too thought it looked as if the female brain was the better brain.

Neither the way the girl does things nor the way the guy does things is better—they're just different. And the key is: *The differences actually complement each other.* When you and a young man get to know each other well, there's sometimes a push in you to make the other person be like you. Unconsciously you might think, "If I can get him to be more like me, life will be easier." The better way to go is to see who the other is, with both of you adapting to the differences so that you can be like a hand in a glove rather than two gloves. (In fact, when you look at mature relationships, relationships that last and relationships in which love is expressed in a happy, healthy way, you'll see that the two lovers measure their maturity by how they accept the other person for who he or she is, not how they try to get the other person to change.)

She might be better at instantaneously seeing the emotions of a situation, like with their friends who need help. He might be better at instantaneously acting to solve the problem of the moment, whether that problem is a sudden fight that's occurring or just what the group ought to do tonight. Both strengths are needed in the life of a couple.

She might be better at doing one kind of complex mental activity in school, but he might be better at another. Let's say they want to start a club in their school. Working together from each other's strengths, they're most likely to get it off the ground and going well.

She might be moodier because she's got so much more going on emotionally, and he might, at that moment, be able to be the steady one because he doesn't have as much access, at that moment, to a river of emotions.

On and on this list goes, flowing from these pages into what you are experiencing in your life. You may be the girl who's better at math than her boyfriend, or the girl who doesn't like to talk about feelings but her boyfriend does, or the girl who hates being interrupted during a task and has a boyfriend who can do three things at once. Life is so filled with variety that we can never say everything is one way, or that whatever way you are or he is, is inferior or superior.

This is where we ended up in the discussion group at the boys' school. Most people in the room admitted to having experienced a lot of the differences we've looked at so far in this book. Most people in the room agreed that caring about each other as males and females requires us to acknowledge that the differences do exist. We ended up deciding that it was okay for guys to be better at some things needed at one moment, and girls to be better at something else needed at another given moment. And we decided being equal did not mean we had to be exactly the same.

From there came the kind of discussion that this chapter focuses on. Given that the differences do exist, how do we relate to each other and get the love we need from each other? If, so often, our brains, our hormones, and therefore our socialization are all pretty different, how do we manage the differences, talk about them, live with them? How do we love and communicate with each other?

To answer these questions, I am now going to go through a number of situations and give advice to you as a girl who is trying to relate to a boy. In giving this advice, I'm going to assume that you agree with me that at least some of the differences I've brought up are real and true; that you have experienced them being with boys you know.

If right now you're thinking, "Duh! Why's he telling *me* this? He should be telling this to the guys I know," understand that I *do* tell boys exactly what I'm telling you. For every topic covered in this chapter, like respecting each other, learning how to talk about your troubles, dealing with violence, I've worked to get boys to take complete responsibility for their part in the puzzle of relationships, too.

THE MATURITY DIFFERENCE

Jeannie was a seventeen-year-old who dated guys in their twenties. When I asked her about the age difference, she said, "I'm more mature than most of the guys my age. I want to be with someone mature."

Jeannie's experience is not unusual. Girls do often mature before boys. You may have started to go through the changes of puberty a year or two earlier than most of the boys around you. And in emotional areas, girls most often mature earlier, as we discussed before.

I'm a guy and I don't consider it an insult to say that, when I was sixteen, sixteen-year-old girls I knew were more mature than I was. It's just the way Mother Nature and society tend to set life up.

When we talk about "maturity difference" here we are mainly talking about emotional maturity. If we were talking about certain kinds of social maturity, we could easily say guys mature earlier—for instance, guys tend to get out and away from the family earlier than girls do; they tend to become independent earlier than girls do; and they tend to try to earn a living earlier than many girls do. So girls don't have all the maturity advantages, but in the emotional area, which is what comes into play most in teen guy/girl relationships, girls often have the maturity advantage.

It's important to remember, if you really care about a guy who is less mature than you are, then you have to work hard not to impose your "adult" expectations on this guy. He is doing the best he can with what nature has given him and society has taught him. You can encourage him to mature—talk more about his feelings, even take on more responsibility in your relationship—but you can't *make* him behave differently and you can't *control* him. You can say, "It hurts me that I'm the one who keeps calling you, and I'm more concerned about how our relationship is going. When you don't pay as much attention to making our relationship work, I feel like you don't really like me deep down." You can say what you feel, but you can't make him feel any differently than he does.

If you do try to control him, you become like

his mother, and he'll resent you. If you've fallen in love with a late-maturing boy, you will need patience, and you will need to identify the things about him you really like—maybe he doesn't care much about what other people think of him—maybe he has that kind of courage—or maybe he's a genius in some things and totally incompetent in others. You just have to completely enjoy these things.

GUYS AND THEIR MOMS

Every teenager has to separate psychologically from his or her mother. This is about deciding we are adults and don't need our mothers to keep us safe and tell us we're okay. It is about pulling away from our mothers, a psychological process that happens over a period of years. And of course, we do the same with our fathers.

Do any of these remarks sound familiar?

"Mom, I'll do it my way!"

"Dad, you don't know me! Back off!"

"Dad, Mom, I love you but you have to let me alone now."

Guys often have an extra hard job in separating from their mothers, and you, as a girlfriend, can get caught in the middle of it.

A teenage boy has to become a man, and his mother can't make him into a man. Teen boys always need their moms to love and support them, but guys have to do a lot of the "becoming men" themselves, with the help of a lot of strong, responsible, fatherly men.

Many of the guys you know may have dads who are working all the time or divorced and therefore not around much. These boys also may not have any or enough trusted men around—like grandfathers or mentors—who spend a lot of time with them on an individual basis, teaching them what being a man is all about. The absence of these fathers and men can stunt a guy's ability to mature.

These boys start the normal psychological separation from their mother before, during, and after puberty—they push against Mom, "tell her off," stop talking to her as much. But they don't have the safety net of close fathers, mentors, or other trusted men to help them take the next step in growing up. And so, very often, girls and girlfriends become the substitute. It falls to you to teach a son how to get away from his mother. You become the main person he turns to (usually without him consciously realizing he's doing this) in order to feel okay about himself as a man. But you are just starting to grow up yourself, and so this puts you in a very difficult position. You become responsible for the self-image of a boy or young man who is very vulnerable, and doesn't even realize he is. He will not only expect you to help him feel good about himself, but, at times, he will also make you into his mother, so that he can get mad at you. Here's how this process called "projection" works.

Let's say you and your boyfriend are with a group and there's some conflict in the group.

Your boyfriend gets into a fight with another guy, then it's over, but maybe you don't like how it ended up and you say to your boyfriend, "Don't you think you ought to say you're sorry?" Your boyfriend might get way more mad at you than you think seems reasonable. Very likely he is reacting this way because he's seeing you as his mother. He's projecting his mother onto you.

Projection is like looking at a photo of someone and superimposing a second photo on top of it. As you separate from your father's authority, you will probably be projecting your father onto your boyfriend more than you realize. We all do some projecting at times.

If you watch adult couples fight, you'll often see lots of this projection. From the outside, what they're fighting about doesn't look like a big deal, but to them it is. That's because the fight they are having is really with their moms or dads or other authority figures whom they've brought into the room like a ghost and super-imposed on their lovers.

Ask your psychology teacher about projection, and watch for it with guys. But remember: Telling a boy he's projecting usually will make him even more mad, at least if you point it out right at the time you're fighting. It's better to be patient, step back, notice how you yourself are probably projecting too, and let the emotional moment pass until maybe it can be discussed later.

There is really nothing you can do about pro-jection, or mother-son separation, except be patient at the moments of trouble, then try to talk to your boyfriend about them later. A day later, you might say, "Yesterday when we were fighting I think for a few seconds I thought you were acting just like my dad, who won't ever apologize—he always thinks he's right. Maybe I got onto you about apologizing partly because of that. And then when I got onto you, do you remember how mad you got? Didn't you maybe think I was being like your mom, telling you what to do?"

Often, teens don't know about "psychological separation from parents" because adults haven't told them about it. You can become a friend who learns with your boyfriend about how this process works.

HANDLING A BOY'S ANGER

I recently worked with a young woman in her late teens, Sandy, who had a boyfriend, Eddie, in his early twenties. He sometimes got very angry. He hit things, he broke things. He had not hit her or their recently born baby, but she was very scared of him.

The first thing I did was talk to the couple together. I had to make sure Sandy was really telling the truth about her boyfriend never hitting her or the child. If he was doing that (or if she was hitting him), then authorities had to get involved. No one should ever put up with another person hitting him or her. *Ever.*

Once we established that he wasn't hitting people, just things, we got to work. We came to understand something about boys, men, and anger that every girl needs to know.

Here's what was happening. During Eddie's day at work, something made him angry. Later, he'd come home. He would walk around the apartment in a dark mood. He wasn't hitting anything yet, he was just depressed. In Sandy's words, "He became dark and scary."

This is where she made a mistake almost all girls make when they care about this kind of person. She wanted his dark mood to go away, or she wanted to fix it. She didn't want to be around him while he was in one of these dark moods because they scared her too much. Sandy also felt unloved and abandoned by him at these times. So she asked him questions about what was bothering him, tried to get him to talk about it, tried to get him closer to her, tried to get him to open up. Instead of dealing with her own fear herself, she tried to get him to become different.

Trying to fix him, trying to make him open up, trying to get his mood finished quickly, had the opposite effect from what she wanted. Almost every time he hurt or hit furniture, the act of hitting came *after* she had pressed at him to talk. I pointed this out to both of them, and both their faces lit up. Neither the young man nor the young woman realized the dance they'd been doing. As they worked to fix it, they developed a new way of doing things. When Eddie got dark or angry, Sandy said nothing, letting him work it out for himself. She thought about how scared he must be to get so dark and so angry. And she also realized the best way to help him—and herself—was to let him be for a while. He didn't need a "mother" telling him what to do, and he didn't need a lover who got herself scared of him; he needed a friend who gave him the space to calm himself down.

It may sound simple, but often the hardest thing to do is nothing. If you just wait and let the mood pass, sometimes, later, a boy can talk about what was bothering him. As a relationship develops over a few years, a couple gradually learns ways of coping with each other's anger, using conflict to make the relationship stronger. But very often, in a young couple's relationship that may not even be a few years old yet, challenging an angry person is something we do because we are scared, and when we do it for this reason, the relationship almost always gets worse, not better.

RESPECT: HOW TO GET IT AND HOW TO GIVE IT

Everyone, guy or girl, needs respect. When national magazine polls ask teens what they want more of in their lives, high on the list and sometimes at the very top is "RESPECT."

Since we're looking at how to relate to boys, let's look at a particularly "male" way of needing respect.

Boys and men are built and socialized to be good at performing—in sports, or the arts, or academics, or in relationships, or all of the above. Testosterone is a hormone that pushes boys to get out there and *do, do, do*. While every boy may go through a lazy phase, still his self-image will be based to a great extent on how he *does* certain things really well.

You might want to identify several things your boyfriend is trying to do really well. If you can help him feel good about himself in these areas, your relationship with him will probably be a stronger one. He will feel respected in the areas where he especially needs respect, and will probably return that respect to you. If you get to feeling things are one-sided—if, for instance, you're encouraging him in his school-work, athletics, arts, friendships, but he's not encouraging you, remind him of what you're doing. Show him how you've been encouraging him, and ask him to give some of this back. Often guys just need to be reminded to encourage other people with words. Often it doesn't come to them as naturally as it might to you.

TEASING: HOW MUCH IS TOO MUCH

All of us, especially during adolescence, like to tease and diss each other. But remember how much it can hurt? Often boys are very hurt by it but don't say anything and store up anger and pain. Without realizing it, you may be teasing your boyfriend in a hurtful way. This is worth watching out for, especially if you're teasing him a lot about the things he's really trying to do well. He might be working very hard on a project in school. Maybe you don't like that it takes him away from you. So, you tease and diss him about it. He doesn't say what he's feeling, but things start to go weird in your relationship.

By the same token, sometimes guys tease girls about the things they want respect for, and unless a girl says, "Hey, that one's off limits for a while!" he doesn't know to leave it alone. Just as you're paying attention to protecting him in places where he's feeling vulnerable, often you have to help him see how to protect you.

MIND READING

Love and teen relationships are magical, but they are not so magical that we can read each other's minds. We are just too different to always know what another person is thinking. There will certainly be moments of intuition where you "just know what he's about to say." There will be times when you finish each other's sentences. There will be times when you both read the same poem and think of each other. All this makes for the magic of love. But these moments also can trick you into thinking that a relationship should be like this most of the time.

Males and females are so different biologically—to say nothing of our different individual personalities and backgrounds—that you can't expect someone to read your mind, and you can't expect to read his. Have you ever heard someone say (or have you yourself said): "If you loved me, you'd know what I'm thinking"? Or: "If you really cared about me, you'd just know the answer to that." This is a crippling and dangerous way to think. What you are really saying is: "Unless you live in my head, you don't love me." Wrong! And even if someone could live in your head, would you like that? You'd have no privacy, no freedom.

Guys often tell me how much girls want them to anticipate their needs. Girls tell me the same about guys. As much as possible, don't fall into this trap. Tell the guy what you need.

"I need you to give me flowers once in a while."

"I need you to call when you say you will. If you're not going to call, don't say you will."

"I need you to tell me when I've done something that makes you feel weird, not just get mad and quiet about it."

You need to tell the guy what you need, but you can't expect that he necessarily can or will give it to you. Being in love is a negotiation, and we never get everything we need from one person. The starting point, however, is to have the strength to say what we need.

Do you find that you seem to know your boyfriend better than he knows you? Do you think you seem to see his emotions better than he sees them himself? Well, you may be right. You may be more emotionally alert than your boyfriend.

But whatever you do, don't keep telling him what you know about him! He'll resent it, and push you away. The wisest person is often the person who knows a truth and acts on it, without having to call attention to the truth itself. If you know something for sure about his emotions, act on your knowledge in some way that helps both of you. Then, later, it may be easier to talk to him about it. Maybe you know he's really nervous about something he has to do, like go for a summer job interview. You know because he's getting upset easily, even picking little fights. Maybe you realize he's trying to push you away with these little fights. Maybe you're tempted to say, "You can't take me being close to you when you're so nervous, can you?" Maybe that will work, but maybe you say it to him and he gets really mad. So, instead of telling him how well you understand what he's going through, maybe you think of something you can do with him that he'll totally enjoy, and you set the whole thing up and surprise him.

Sometimes, sneaking in the back door is a lot easier than pushing in through the front.

VIOLENCE

We've talked about how boys are often more physically aggressive than girls. And on the other side, we've talked about how girls are often more emotionally articulate, and so can be verbally manipulative. If either of these tendencies isn't held in check, it can result in violence. Either the boy or the girl has gone too far in verbal or physical aggression (something that happens very often when one or both have been drinking).

People these days like to talk about violence as something we need only worry about from teen boys and men. When you hear lectures on domestic violence or sexual harassment, it's common to hear solely about the part the boy or man plays. Watch out during these sorts of discussions. While boys and men can be violent, so can girls and women. Sometimes these discussions forget that even though the boy hits harder, he doesn't always hit first.

Have you ever slapped a boy? If you haven't, you've probably known a girl who has. A girl slapping a boy is considered a little romantic, whereas a boy slapping or hitting a girl is considered a crime. We're smartest when we consider any physical act of anger an act of violence and a crime—whether it's a slap like in the movies or a fist in the face.

Maybe you've never hit a boy, but have you ever cut a boyfriend down to size with words? Have you watched him become deeply ashamed—maybe even so red-faced you thought he would do something violent? Girls often are able to use words so quickly, so devastatingly, that boys, who often can't process or defend themselves as well verbally, turn to the one thing they have left, their fists. If you cut your boyfriend down a lot, you're being violent too.

I've said these same things to boys, too. Boys are not allowed to hit or cut down their girlfriends. If anybody is doing this, he or she ought to get help fast from an adult they trust.

GETTING HIM TO TALK

You probably know many ways to get your boyfriend to talk about what is going on in his life—what's bothering him, what matters to him. Let me add these methods to what you already know.

- Boys often respond to "What do you think?" better than "What do you feel?"
- You often can help a conversation by filling in emotional words. "Are you feeling sad? Are you feeling angry? Are you feeling afraid? Are you feeling hurt?" These are "sentence stems" to which you can add people, places, and things. For instance, "Are you feeling hurt because my mother didn't ask you to dinner?" "Are you feeling angry about what John said about how you played in the band last night?" Sad, hurt, angry, sad, afraid, joyful, happy, lonely... these are "feeling names." Filling them in can help boys figure out their feelings.

Does your boyfriend cut you off whenever you try to talk about your feelings? Some boys can't seem to be cured of this—they are so afraid of your feelings. The fact is relationships with them can't last; they just aren't mature enough to carry on emotional conversation.

To get talking about personal issues with guys, you often need to talk very concretely, tell shorter stories, and stop yourself more frequently to get feedback. Remember that the male brain often finds long emotional conversations very confusing, especially the kind a lot of girls are good at—conversations that take into account things that happened years ago to people the guy never met.

This is the area of a relationship that is perhaps the most out of balance—that girls tend to want so much more emotional conversation than boys. It is a problem that is not solved by girls getting mad at boys or by boys being impatient and domineering with girls. It is solved by women and men, girls and boys, all over the world in the same way: compromise. She changes the way she talks, he changes the way he listens. As with all important things in life, the wise way of doing it is simple.

- You talk, he gives feedback. After that, he can talk if he wishes, and you give feedback.

- Don't rely on your boyfriend for more than about thirty or forty percent of your emotional needs. Stay close to your family—as much as possible—and your girlfriends and other friends so that you have a lot of places to go to talk and to be heard and to be cared about. Your boyfriend is only your boyfriend, right? He's not your whole world. When it feels like he is your whole world, know that it's mainly your hormones talking. For a few weeks or months

it's fun to have physical attraction rule your life, but real love begins when the hormones give way to something deeper and you see more about how to relate to this guy, how to fit him into *your* life.

DECIDING ABOUT SEX

Have we saved the best for last? Sex! Let's talk about it.

This is an area where the differences between boys and girls are so big and so important, and yet our parents, our communities, and our cultures teach us so very little.

I'm going to focus on male/female differences now, even though we all know that a lot of what girls and boys want and need from sex is the same.

Boys tend to want sex more and girls tend to want "relationship" more. Right? Sometimes not—there are certainly girls who want and enjoy lots of sex—but for the most part yes. Studies from all over the world on the amount of sex that teens and adults have show us the same results—the average male from puberty on into old age has more sexual intercourse and masturbates more than the average female.

Think of it this way: Males carry in them trillions of potentially fertile sperm. Females carry in their lifetime around three hundred potentially fertile eggs. The biological drive of those trillions of sperm is greater than that of the three hundred eggs.

Girls may get horny at any time, but their hormones go through cycles in which girls don't feel horny at all. You've felt these dull, low, moody, angry times. Sex is the last thing on your mind. You've also felt what it's like to have your "horniness" hormone surge; it's often right around your time of ovulation, or fertility.

The adolescent male body, on the other hand, is getting five to seven spikes in his testosterone level per day. Where you may masturbate once a week, a teen boy may do it once a day.

So, very often, sexually active teens find that the male wants sex more than the female. The biological reasons aren't just hormonal. The female body is set up to be selective about who it has sex with. A female is biologically driven to find a male whom she can trust to take care of her three hundred potentially fertile eggs. The male body is set up to have sex with any female it's attracted to, because its biological job is to get to one of those eggs and fertilize it.

Among adults, males have more extramarital affairs than females. Among teens, males, on average, start becoming sexually active a year before females do.

On and on the differences go. There's a lot

going on besides sexual biology. Culture certainly plays a part, telling girls to be virgins and guys to "play around." But most of what culture does is to reinforce its interpretation of the biology.

When to Start Being Sexually Active. Biology holds a key to the problems that arise over the question of sex for adolescents, and biology is also the key to a lot of the solutions.

When thinking about a sexual relationship, a young woman definitely ought to make sure the guy is trustworthy enough to care for her very few and very sacred eggs. It goes without saying that, in these times when sexually transmitted diseases are prevalent, every sexually active teen should be using birth control and practicing safe sex. Still, a young woman should think about intercourse in terms of its most serious and wonderful potential—to make a child. How will she know if a guy is trustworthy? The answer is she must get to know him for a long period of time before considering intercourse.

What is wrong with a girl being in a relationship with a guy for a year or two before she decides he is trustworthy enough to have intercourse with? What is wrong with her waiting till she's married to the guy, if that's what her religion or values encourage her to do? Absolutely nothing. Unless she cuts the guy off from sex completely. Besides denying her own needs, she's not taking into account his needs—the needs of a testosterone-surging adolescent male.

As always, compromise is key. There are many ways to have sex without vaginal intercourse. If you are thinking about becoming sexually active, you might consider enjoying your body and your boyfriend's body with mutual oral sex and mutual masturbation. Make your sex life beautiful and fun but never feel compelled to have vaginal intercourse with anyone. There's a difference between all the various kinds of "sex" and "sexual intercourse."

Now, I'm one of those very "sensitive" males, good at talking about my feelings, and very involved in the life of feelings and emotions. At the same time, I remember that when I was fifteen, sixteen, seventeen, eighteen, I could use "feelings" to get sex if I wanted it. I remember saying, "I love you," and "You're the most beautiful girl in the world," and "There will never be anyone like you." I was using emotional words but often mainly because I wanted sex in return for those words. I also remember a very wise girl of seventeen saying to me, "I want to stay a virgin until I'm married, but here are some things we can do." She showed me a thing or two! I respected her—though I was irritated by her resistance at first—and we had a very good relationship, sexual and otherwise.

Getting It Done. During sex, the male is, in general, propelled biologically toward the act of ejaculation (and what leads up to ejaculation). He's less directed toward emotional conversation and physical connection (like hugging, caressing, kissing), which is what females often want more of—before, during, and after sex. Guys see a lot of this stuff as "not important" because it doesn't lead toward ejaculation.

If you're sexually active and you've noticed this difference—he doesn't want as much foreplay or cuddling afterward as you do—you're noticing something very normal, something males and females experience all over the world. Once the male body ejaculates, it is often done. The hugging, cuddling, and talking that might follow the sex act is far more often initiated by the female than by the male, often to her great frustration. Beforehand, he might even say, "Yes, yes, I love you," and mean, "Let's get to the sex and ejaculation part soon, please."

It takes months, sometimes years, for couples to resolve this frustration. Be patient with this one. Some couples are married for decades and this problem is never resolved completely. Be vigilant, listen carefully, use your intuition about whether you are really and truly loved. And don't be surprised if six months into the relationship with a guy you find that he himself is changing—that six months ago he said "I love you" to get sex, but now he really means "I love you."

Sex Objects: Myths and Reality. Relationships between young men and women can get wrecked because of a guy's hardwired (and culturally amplified) tendency to see girls and young women as sex objects. Remember that male sexual biology drives a guy to spend at least some of his internal energy on being constantly on the lookout for a female who is attractive and carries potentially fertile eggs. A guy whose eyes stray to another pretty, sexy girl risks the anger of his girlfriend. He is considered emotionally immature because he has just turned his head and watched an attractive female "object" move through space. You, his girlfriend, may very well pull away from him, offended and hurt.

While, in some cases, adolescent boys look at other girls just to do a number on their girlfriend, or because they aren't really committed to their girlfriend, very often much of his "looking" is a quick, non-emotional reflex of biology.

One college student of mine said something very telling about this. "I was explaining to my girlfriend that it doesn't mean anything when I look at someone else. It's just me enjoying a pretty girl. Telling her that is like telling her I've slept with someone else. She hates me for a week. I told her I didn't want to be controlled, I'll look where I want. She called me a kid who can't grow up."

In working with young people and helping them understand relationships, I teach them how the brain works so girls won't condemn a "look" as immature. I also teach the males to learn to control their impulse to "look" when they are with their girlfriends. And I help guys learn that the line between a "look" and a sexual insult or come-on is not a line to cross.

Since we're talking about these "looks" boys often make (and girls do it too, right?), let's just mention how different sexual fantasies can be for guys and girls. Boys definitely spend on average more time fantasizing about sex than girls do. This is part of the package when you are involved with a guy sexually. He may want to try "weird" things and may talk about "weird" dreams or fantasies. Most of this is very normal. (Of course, if you're ever uncomfortable, you have to say that.) Most of the time, instead of being scared of your boyfriend's quick looks at other girls, or by his sexual fantasies, why not talk to him about them? Ask him what they are. It can become an amazing and courageous conversation in which you two might become even closer than you were.

In all the points we've covered in this chapter, one thing we can never say enough is this: Listen to your intuition, and always have trusted adults to talk to about these things. You and your boyfriend, even you and your girlfriends, just can't work some of this stuff out without the help of the adults who love and care about you. Trust your parents, or if you can't talk to them right now, make sure you have an aunt, or grandmother, or teacher, or other "mentor" to help you learn how to communicate better with the boys you care about. Part of what these trusted elders will do is to trust you back. Hopefully, they'll answer your questions with: "Well, what does your intuition tell you?" Throughout your life, that intuition will be your wisest counsel.

Afterword

When I was a teen, I sure wanted someone to explain more about girls. Maybe I wouldn't always have agreed with everything I was told, but I know I'd have learned a lot.

I hope I've helped you understand boys better. I know you may not agree with everything I've said, but I hope you have a deeper, clearer picture of boys now.

When I was starting this book, I asked my wife her opinion on what ought to go in it. She said, "Well, what would you want to teach your daughters when they get to high-school age?" (My daughters are now six and nine.) I loved my wife's question, and I've tried to answer it in this book.

If you want to keep understanding more

about young men and how you, as a young woman, can get along with them, let me suggest some more books to read.

To understand teen males better, try my adult books *A Fine Young Man* and *The Wonder of Boys*.

To understand how couples work, try Harville Hendrix's *Getting the Love You Want*, Patricia Love's *Hot Monogamy*, and John Gray's *Men Are from Mars, Women Are from Venus*.

To understand more about girls, try *Have You Started Yet?*, by Ruth Thomson, a book on female biology, and Mary Pipher's *Reviving Ophelia*, a book about the traps teen girls often get into.

To understand more about how male brains and female brains can be so different, try *Brain Sex* by Anne Moir and David Jessel and *Sex on the Brain* by Deborah Blum.

If this book has interested you, show it to your teachers and schools. I hope one day every school and community starts really talking openly about boys and girls and the challenges they face as teens.

Thanks for reading.
Good luck to you.

Michael Gurian
P.O. Box 8714
Spokane, WA 99203
www.michael-gurian.com

A BOOK FOR THE
PARENTS AND TEACHERS
OF ADOLESCENT BOYS

Michael Gurian's
A Fine Young Man

A *New York Times*
Bestseller

"This book is filled with stories and practical advice for parents and teachers of adolescent boys. Michael Gurian takes a thoughtful look at nature and nurture, and at the role of culture and testosterone in the lives of boys. I recommend it to all who want to raise fine young men."

—Mary Pipher, author of *Reviving Ophelia*

"*A Fine Young Man* convincingly illustrates. . . the peculiar pain and potential loneliness of being a boy in America today."

—*Time*

"Proactive and ultimately imbued with hope. With persuasive eloquence, Gurian outlines thoughtful and practical steps"

—*Publishers Weekly* (starred review)

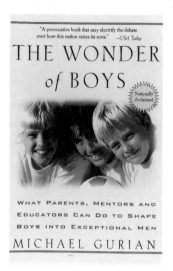

ALSO BY MICHAEL GURIAN

The Wonder of Boys: What Parents, Mentors and Educators Can Do to Shape Boys into Exceptional Men

THE NATIONAL BESTSELLER

"*The Wonder of Boys* became the impetus for a growing 'boys movement'..."

—*USA Today*

"Full of good insights and advice."
—*Los Angeles Times*

"*The Wonder of Boys* will help future generations open the lines of communication between men and women by giving us what we need to raise strong, responsible, and sensitive men."

—John Gray, author of *Men Are from Mars, Women Are from Venus*